This Little Tiger book belongs to:

_____

_____

_____

To my two children,
Luke and Hayley
~ *PK*

To Raechele and Jim
~*JC*

Little Tiger Press
An imprint of Magi Publications
1 The Coda Centre, 189 Munster Road, London SW6 6AW
www.littletigerpress.com

First published in Great Britain 2002
This edition published 2003

Printed in Belgium by Proost NV

PETER KAVANAGH

JANE CHAPMAN

Love
Like
This

LITTLE TIGER PRESS

LONDON

The pale sun rises through morning mist.
We go walking together on days like this.

When storm winds blow we shelter together. Nothing can harm us while we have each other.

Later we chase across hot dusty plains,
stomping and stamping and playing new games.

When the bright sun rises
hotter and higher, we stride along
by the cool fast river.

The water is clean and we're covered in dust. We jump in together and let it wash over us.

We dip and dive and splash and splish.
Fun like this is all we could wish.

We walk in the grass to dry in the sun
and sing together in trumpeting fun.

Sometimes we laugh for no reason at all,
comparing our trunks, one big, one small.

We gaze at the birds flying into the night
and the stars in the sky, all twinkly and bright.

And when we lie in the soft dewy grass,
you tell me elephant tales from the past.

Last thing at night we curl in a hug,
safe and happy, cosy and snug.

And we sink into sleep and dream of new days.
Love like this is love always.

More stories to share from Little Tiger Press

The Very Sleepy Sloth
Andrew Murray
Jack Tickle

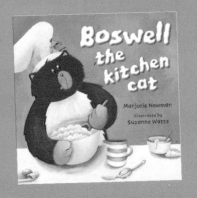

Boswell the kitchen cat
Marjorie Newman
Illustrated by Suzanne Watts

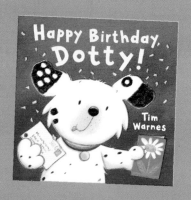

Happy Birthday, Dotty!
Tim Warnes

Pigs Can't Fly!
Ben Cort

Ready for Bed!
Jane Johnson
Illustrated by Gaby Hansen

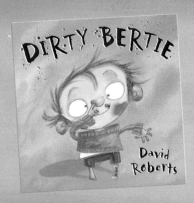

Dirty Bertie
David Roberts

For information regarding any of the above titles
or for our catalogue, please contact us:
Little Tiger Press,
1 The Coda Centre, 189 Munster Road,
London SW6 6AW
Tel: 020 7385 6333 Fax: 020 7385 7333
E-mail: info@littletiger.co.uk
www.littletigerpress.com